A Very Sisterly Murder

A Phoenix Detective Mystery
Book #1

Shelly Young Bell

ii

To Dick and Kate

This is a work of fiction. It is not biographical nor autobiographical. All names, characters, places, and incidents are the product of the author's imagination or are used fictitiously, and any resemblance to actual persons living or dead, places or events is entirely coincidental.

Shelly Young Bell

The Phoenix Detective Mysteries
A Very Sisterly Murder, Book 1
Murder at St. Katherine's, Book 2
The Diamond Dunes Murders, Book 3
The Cabot College Murders, Book 4
Population 10, The Dead End Murders, Book 5
R.S.V.P. to Murder, Book 6
Murder on the Promenade Deck, Book 7
Murder at 13 Curves, Book 8

Historic Novel
Stand Like the Brave

Copyright © 2019 Shelly Young Bell
Revised / Updated 2022
All Rights Reserved
ISBN-13: 9781096017493

Shelly Young Bell

Ann Essex and police associate Bill Dancer Spend the weekend at a Pennsylvania Dutch Bed Inn. Will the surfacing of an abusive lover from her past drive Ann to murder? Can she keep her daughter, Robin, safe from this maniac? Will she be able to escape the weekend with her mother, sisters and nieces without having to expose her past to her new colleague?

Follow Detective Ann Essex, her associate Detective Bill Dancer, best friends Suzanne and Che-Che, and investigative daughter Robin as they solve murders and piece together the mysteries they encounter.

Shelly Young Bell

Chapter 1

Prologue

I sat in the car and opened the manila envelope. I hoped when I reviewed the photos of the victim they would be "before" shots and not "after" shots. Luckily, this time, they had been taken before the murder, before the brutal knifing and beating. I studied the honey blond hair swept back off the pert young face.

Pictures in hand, I got out of my car and went into the burger barn, to begin the search for her identity and the search for the last person to see her alive – her murderer. I didn't know how lucky this first stop would prove to be. Or how unlucky.

"She comes in every week, right as rain, at about 7:15, always orders a large coffee. Reads a novel. A Dick Francis novel. I wondered 'why' the first few weeks. But then I guess I just got used to her coming in. Regular, like. Coffee and a mystery for an evening. A different novel every week. I took

to noticing that. What the titles were, I mean. I wondered how many novels the man had written. How many Tuesdays would they last? Would she still come in after she'd finished reading everything he had written, or would she switch to a different author? Of course, I only think about her at 7:15 Tuesdays. When she actually comes in.

"She's a string of pearls kind of girl. I could tell that straight off. Navy blue wool coat, low black heals. Very nice. Very pleasant. Sleek hair, not that straggly never-combed look. Not for her."

I let the manager talk. HARRIS, his nametag said. Was HARRIS his first name, or his last name, I wondered. Attractive fellow, reddish hair, a look about him that probably meant he had been given to lots of freckles as a kid. This probably was it for him -- burger barn manager. But I could see he was good at it. Even as he talked to me, he had one eye on the kids working the counter and the grill behind us, making sure they did their jobs, and that his kingdom was at its best.

"She comes in about 7:15 every Tuesday. Yep, that's her," he finished, handing the photo back to me.

"Seen her recently?" I asked, knowing full well she hadn't had her coffee and good read this week. Instead, sometime Monday morning she had been savagely mauled. Killed almost instantly with a blow to the head, then beaten and slashed. Disgusting, but that was my neck of the woods.

A Very Sisterly Murder

"No, not this week," he tried to smile, "What's she done?"

I smiled unsuspiciously back. He'd realize soon enough. Guess he hadn't seen the papers yet. "Nothing, just need to locate her. Thanks."

"Yep, String of Pearls at 7:15, the homeless guy at 7:30. Can always count on them on Tuesdays. Lots of regulars come in here. You know, like after a night class at the college up the road there, maybe working late once a week, or having their kid out for a burger."

"Yeah? Anyone that this girl used to talk to, sit with, show any interest in?" I asked. I saw him hesitate, not knowing if he should actually say or speculate. Sometimes people hesitated -- afraid of saying something that would appear incriminating. It was always in their eyes -- that somewhat unfocused look for a second or two, as if they were transported away and then brought back -- recalling, evaluating, deciding.

He was back.

"Well, not what you would call 'friendly', but once she asked me about the homeless guy, about if he ever actually eats anything. I told her that all he has is a cup of coffee like she does. He always has money to pay for it, but it is my policy that he can eat anytime he comes in and doesn't have the money for it. He knows it, too."

"Homeless guy?"

"Well, you know, like a bum, carrying a bag or two of stuff with him. Thin, hairy, dirty. Actually,

he comes in with such regularity I suspect he has a place close by. He comes in, drinks a coffee, smokes a cigar, colors on a paper a little bit, nods to my workers. Harmless fellow. I feel sorry for him in a way. They never speak to each other, but she seems to be concerned for him."

"And he comes in every Tuesday as well?"

"Yes."

"Here's my card, if you think of anything else about the girl, please call me here, will you?"

HARRIS looked at my card. Tucked it in his shirt pocket behind his name tag.

I would have to look for this homeless guy and check every nook and cranny of this girl's life to find the clues needed to lead to the arrest and then the conviction of her murderer. That was my bailiwick. I was good at routing out the concrete facts, the all-convicting facts. No jury had ever set a man free that I had investigated and arrested. The department knew I was good, turned a blind eye to my antics when necessary, and had successfully kept me at the rank of Detective so I could do the investigating. No upstairs desk job for me. I wouldn't want them to know it, but this was the way I wanted it. Pay, prestige, title -- keep it. I wanted the hunt.

A Very Sisterly Murder

Chapter 2

Bill Dancer rolled the paper up out of the old Smith Corona typewriter and eyed his words. He smiled, happy with his effort, his slight dimples showing on his clean-shaven face. He absent-mindedly smoothed his short dark hair with one hand. He rolled the paper back down, lined up the type with the little metal keys, and waited. He was aware of the thin October afternoon light coming in his one office window. But this wouldn't be his office for long. The wall clock click-clicked away each second. Distracted by the noise, he fidgeted, tapping his strong fingers on the desk, then taking a swig of his now cold black coffee.

He glanced at the clock. Two-twenty. Not time yet. Not time to call it a day, leave this job and enter the new world of Bill Dancer, *Big City* Detective. He was leaving this job, this office, this small town and heading east to Philadelphia to his new job. Out of this small town and its mundane crimes, and to the big city where he could better use the skills he'd acquired these last ten years.

It was a long drive and he was heading out very shortly. He'd be spending the weekend at the Garnet Inn; a quiet, transitional weekend about halfway to Philadelphia. Just him and his writing. Then Sunday afternoon, having fortified himself with the big brunch at the Inn, he'd drive the rest of the way to arrive at his new apartment with the single carload of possessions he was taking along. Monday would be soon enough to focus on real murder and mayhem. The weekend was his, and his alone. a rare commodity in police work.

Just the thought made his heart race. Time alone to write. If his co-workers had known, he'd had been the laughing stock of the local police department. No problem, he just hadn't told them. But still, he knew it was pretty sad to be almost thirty, and the most exciting thing he could think of to do on his first weekend off in weeks was to spend it alone at a country inn, writing. He looked at the clock again. Two-twenty-two. Still too early to leave. He looked out the window again, not liking the way the weak yellow light filtered through the thickening gray sky. Ominous. Too still, too fragile. Weather was coming. He wanted to hit the road before the weather got bad.

Rereading what he had typed, Bill stewed on the wisdom of having the homeless man smoking a cigar. Too upscale for a bum? Places his story too concretely in the era before the ban on smoking in restaurants? He'd have to work that detail out another time.

Bill grabbed the paper by its top and pulled it out of the typewriter, opened his black leather portfolio, purchased especially for his new adventure, and slipped the paper into it out of sight of any taunting coworkers. He picked up the old, black, city-issued desk phone.

"Marie, I'm gone. Yeah, you, too, Have a great weekend. It was great working with you. Yeah, I'll send you a postcard from Philly," and hung up. He hated emotional good-byes. Bill straightened his stylish red and blue tie, opened his top left drawer and took out his revolver, checked quickly out of habit to make sure it was loaded and had the safety on, and stuck it into his shoulder holster under a new charcoal gray suit jacket, flipped off the light and left.

No looking back now. This initial detective job had been good to him after his years in a patrol car wearing blue. But the rank of full

A Very Sisterly Murder

Detective with a big city police force was what he had really craved, and had worked hard to attain. His parents had not understood his preoccupation with law enforcement, but had not discouraged him. At seventeen, he could not find the words to adequately explain his decision to go to the police academy instead of the local college as his parents had assumed that he would. He had done well as a police officer and then these last couple of years as a junior level detective, but now it was time to move on to a larger, more urban area where he felt his detecting skills, his penchant for investigating, listening, and sifting through the facts could be of greatest use.

This writing thing – this passion he had for words – well, Bill had no idea from where the words sprang, what depths prompted him to write, to explore the power of words on paper. He had long ago given up questioning the Why of his need to write. Nowadays he found himself concentrating on the When he would find time to write, as his life had become more complicated with work demands.

Some cops drank. Some cops chased women. Some cops took that unthinkable step down into the world of crime they had pledged to fight. Bill – well, he knew his weakness was this urge to put his inner words on paper, and he hoped it would not prove the death of him.

Chapter 3

While driving east on the Pennsylvania Turnpike late that afternoon, the setting sun at his back now red through the thickening clouds, Bill Dancer listened to a tape in his car on the subject of writer's block. He understood his *need* to write – like being possessed, like having a terrible illness, or a drug addiction. He knew the feeling, the impatience with everyday life, the waiting for his own time when he was free to let the words flow. Ignoring the passing of time, and the need for food, he would just write and write until his mind was clouded, fogged with characters and places he'd created there on the paper before him. He was often so tired after working his shift and then getting in a few hours of writing, he'd slump over on his bed and sleep until he had to wake up for his next shift at the local police station.

What he could not quite relate to was this talk of writer's block, or the '100 ways to avoid writing' that other writers seemed so keen on talking about. He usually had no trouble – he just sat down and wrote. It was like a mighty river, always welling and flowing; the currents changed, eddied, swirled, and even if he sometimes found himself off course, it always flowed onward.

A Very Sisterly Murder

One of the ladies in his writer's support group once divulged that she would do anything to postpone putting pen to paper – clean the bathroom, rake the garden, run to the store for milk and bread which they did not need, polish her husband's shoes, anything! Bill was ever so glad he did not experience that affliction. He hoped he would never be in a position to envy these years when the words came easily to him.

Bill switched off the lecture and concentrated on the last part of the drive. The Garnet Inn was just a couple miles off the Turnpike, over an ancient covered bridge, and into the hills just east of Lancaster in Amish country. He let his car go up over the lip onto the bridge gently, proceeding with caution in case the decking was not as secure as it should be. The stream below probably was a fly fisherman's delight, but was this afternoon swollen and the current much faster than would allow a man to stand waist high in it without being swept away. The coming storm would only worsen that. Bill wondered how often the bridge had come close to annihilation as the creek reached flood stage.

Bill had picked this Inn for the quiet ambiance the brochure promised. He had booked a single room, made a dinner reservation in the 1776 Restaurant for seven-thirty that evening, and packed his "country inn weekend" duds. By the time he arrived at four-thirty in the afternoon, the winds had picked up noticeably, and the threat of a nasty thunderstorm swirled overhead like witches in a tempest. He parked out back of the inn, grabbed his suitcase and his briefcase with his writing in it, locked up the old Ford, and headed for the front door.

The Inn appeared old. It was large. He wondered how many rooms they had to let out, how large the public spaces were. Here alone in the woods it seemed immense. Late Victorian, he estimated. He pushed open the front door into the reception area. Not huge, but there was a roaring fire in the fireplace across the room that made up for the size of the room. A couple of ladies lingered about, obviously waiting for others to join them. Bill crossed the old braided rug to the reception desk. A middle age man and women were behind the counter.

"Hi, I have a reservation for tonight and tomorrow night. William Dancer, " he said pleasantly.

"Right, let me just check," the man said, turning to the computer terminal tucked in under the counter, out of sight. He fiddled with it a few minutes.

"Sorry for that delay, wind gets into the wires, and sometimes the computers don't work really well when it gets blustery. Here it is, yes, Mr. William Dancer, two nights, room 212. And a dinner reservation for tonight at seven-thirty. All set. How many keys, one or two?"

"Just one." Bill slid his American Express card across the old oak countertop. The man slid back a key with number 212 showing brightly on the polished brass European style fob. Bill took the key, slid it into his suit coat pocket, and then signed the registration card. Giving the pen back to the man, Bill noticed how agitated the man seemed. The man saw Bill watching him.

"Oh, sorry. We are going to be very busy this weekend. I keep hoping some people decide not to make it as I don't know how we are going to squeeze everyone in. It's a peak color weekend for leaf peeping, and there is a high school class reunion tomorrow -- Class of 1946. So, not only is the Inn full tonight and tomorrow, we have a banquet tomorrow night and will probably be at the maximum dining room capacity both nights. It's homecoming at the high school, so half my day staff will either be at the bonfire and game tonight and in no shape to work tomorrow, or out to the formal dance tomorrow night and in no shape to work Sunday. And now this storm coming, they are saying it could be quite a doozy. Sorry, didn't mean to vent," the man said.

"No problem," Bill answered, "just so long as the sheets are clean, there's hot water for a shower, and ice at the bar. We'll be okay."

A Very Sisterly Murder

The man smiled at Bill's easy way of dealing with it. But Bill knew that the man had a million details to attend to. He must be the owner/manager. Bill figured the woman also behind the counter must be his wife as there was such an easy familiarity between them, the way they moved out of each other's way and looked at each other.

Bill turned, picked up his bags and looked for the stairs. No elevator, but his room was only one flight up. Behind him, busting in through the doors came a large group of women of assorted ages. They were laughing and bubbling over with excitement. He overheard snatches of their conversation as they approached the other women who had been waiting in the lobby, hovering near the fireplace, studying the old porcelains on the mantel.

"Surprise! It's a weekend for your birthday, mom!"

"Surprise, we're all here!"

"Surprise! No, no, the whole weekend is on us, you don't get to pay for anything!"

"Here's Leigh, too! Up from York!"

"Yes, all four of us daughters, and two of the three granddaughters!"

"I figure a lot of looking at quilts, shopping and eating!"

"Surprise!"

Bill Dancer reached the landing of the second floor, out of earshot of the happy ladies downstairs.

Definitely an old place, he thought to himself. The carpets were a bit worn. Faded elegance, but real. The walls were a sooty white. What was that color called, he wondered? All the woodwork and doors were still the original fumed oak. The wide hallway, laid with antique rugs covering the original random width hardwood floors, was dotted with late Victorian furniture, a settee here, a chair there. Bill checked the room number on his key again. 212. He came to the end of the hall where it took a ninety degree turn to the right. There was an open room to his right, a lounge of sorts. He'd have to check that out later. Just before the hallway doglegged to the right, he saw his room. Yes, there it was, 212, on the left. He inserted the key into the door lock and opened the door.

It was a lovely room with a small gilt and crystal chandelier in the center of the high, plastered ceiling. An Edwardian mahogany bed with matching dressers. There was a small writing desk and chair. The room was overall a sedate blue and cream, not the ubiquitous Laura Ashley rose print as he had feared. Perfect, he said to himself. He set his suitcase on the bed and, crossing over to the desk, set his new briefcase down and took a quick look at his watch. Five minutes after five. Just enough time for a quick shower and a change into his dinner clothes before a drink in the downstairs bar and then his dinner reservation in the 1776 Restaurant. He had planned his exit from the stifling small town existence he had endured these last ten years, and this transition weekend of relaxation, comfort and writing before taking up his new life in Philadelphia with great care and deliberation. Some might say obsessive. It might be quite a while before he had the luxury of two whole days of nonstop writing and indulgent leisure, and he wanted every minute to be maximized.

Chapter 4

To have the afternoon off and not be on call for the entire weekend for her mother's 75th birthday celebration weekend, Detective Ann Essex had to call in a few favors from her colleagues with the Philadelphia detectives. But she luckily had had three months' notice, so it was arranged in plenty of time. Ann had tilted her short blond hair at one of the two younger detectives that she had asked to cover for her and looked at him hard with her blue eyes until he succumbed to her request. On the other detective she used her more senior officer tactic, trying to use that tone of voice that conveyed 'if your superior asks, just do it.' Now she just needed to get out the door before any last-minute emergency came up.

Ann shut down her computer, and dropped files off at the appropriate desks on her way out of the office.

"Yeah, see you Monday, Bernadette – if I decide to come back! A weekend in the country might convince me to stay there and chuck all this," Ann laughed and said to her junior associate.

Ann steered the car out of the guarded parking lot and headed across town to the Schuylkill Expressway to King of Prussia and Valley Forge, and then continued west on the Pennsylvania turnpike toward her weekend destination.

Ann had directions to the Garnet Inn taped to the dashboard of her old Corolla, but she had almost two hours of turnpike driving before she would need them. She started to feel the pressures of work and motherhood start to slip away as she drove into the suburbs, then into the countryside dotted with farms, some Amish, some not.

It was to be an adult women's weekend and celebration for her mother's birthday, and although daughter, Robin, was very grown up for being only ten years old, Ann had reluctantly decided that Robin should stay at home this weekend. She didn't want the weekend marred by any childish behavior.

It had been a rough week at the Essex home. Just now, when life seemed so settled and so right, Ann had been given medical news that her eyes were failing and would continue to fail with no cure, no improvement. What she thought had been the signs of needing a new prescription in her glasses now that she was forty, turned out to be seriously bad news. A few tears and an evening of self-pity was all she allowed herself. After all, as she told her husband, John, she could be hit by a bus tomorrow and this eye thing wouldn't mean a thing! John had taken it philosophically as he was wont to do with this type of situation – it was certainly something they could and would deal with as they went forward. Like a phoenix, Ann would rise above whatever ashes, destruction and difficulty this eye problem settled on her, her career, and her homelife. Ann was determined not to let this get her down. She had risen above worse catastrophes than this. She gave herself a small physical shake to stop herself from thinking about it.

John. Ann mused a bit over him – older, steady, quiet, 'the dullest guy she'd ever know' as he described himself. He had been so good to her these last five years since he had married 'them'. He knew that when he married Ann, he was in essence marrying the two of them, taking on Robin as daughter – his, yet not his, a conundrum.

A Very Sisterly Murder

Ann refocused herself back on driving. The winds had picked up, and there were clouds thickening, threatening in the western sky. She hoped she could reach the Inn before it all let loose for the night.

Tonight, there was to be a festive birthday dinner in the colonial themed dining room. Tomorrow the group would travel around to quilt shops, Amish country stores and the local sights for the day. Ann's mom loved to quilt. This weekend was, after all, for her mom. The Inn was located squarely in the middle of Amish quilting land. There would be sights and smells and tastes new to most of her sisters and nieces. Thinking about being here in Pennsylvania Dutch country, Ann started to crave a big slice of gooey and sugary shoofly pie.

Again, Ann pulled herself back from the daydreaming to the task at hand of driving. She drove efficiently and conservatively. Being a cop, she knew how to stay off the radar, literally. Off the Radar – Ann frequently wondered during the last ten years if she *had* managed to do just that in her everyday life.

Securing her Bachelor's Degree from a college on the Main Line of Philadelphia, then off to do graduate work at a nearby university, but eventually fleeing to Scotland to escape a relationship she really didn't want nor knew how to end efficiently, finally taking in infant Robin as her own – she had made big decisions on her own at a young age and often to the surprise of family and friends. Coming home from Scotland not only with her Master's Degree completed but with a baby in tow with little explanation, Ann had taken a job with the police department – good benefits, good pay – a job secured for her by friends in high places, some of whom she did not even know by name. It had been arranged and taken care of by her benefactors in Scotland, probably more to secure Robin's future than her own. She had been grateful for the assistance. It had meant not having to move back in with her parents. As her life had evened out, and she had fallen into living what many considered a normal life, Ann less and less frequently thought about the past. The present and future were enough for her. But she had always kept her eyes and ears open, just in case.

The exit for her first turn appeared on a big green Turnpike sign overhead. Two miles now. She hoped the daylight lasted long enough for her to be able to read her typed out, turn by turn directions. The Corolla was old enough not to have built-in GPS. The type size on the paper was very large, but still Ann looked at it in the growing twilight and wondered if it she would be able to see it. Once through the tolls, Ann headed up the twisty hilly road and slowed to a crawl over an old wooden covered bridge. The car's headlights illuminated the inside of the bridge. Ann wondered how many storms as bad as this one this bridge had survived. She kept a look out for the Garnet Inn. She shouldn't have worried she'd miss it as there was a large wooden sign swinging in the gusty wind marking the driveway.

The Garnet Inn. Ann wondered if all the walls would be a dark red, or if perhaps it was named after Mr. Garnet. Time would tell. Ann had done no research for the weekend, just allowing herself to be immersed into the plans that her youngest sister, Beth, had arranged: the Inn, the rooms, the dinner and the shopping excursion itinerary for Saturday. Sunday would be a final birthday brunch before everyone then headed their separate ways home. The other sisters and nieces had committed to the weekend and gone along with all the plans for the weekend. The sisters had proved to be surprisingly agreeable to let Beth make the decisions, as sometimes over their adult years the four of them had not always been so affable. Ann was glad to just be part of it and not to have been in charge of the whole thing. Ann hoped her mom enjoyed the weekend as much as she knew she would.

A Very Sisterly Murder

Chapter 5

The excitement level was high among the women as they climbed the stairs in search of their rooms. Lynn, the eldest daughter at fifty and dark haired like her mom, had arrived early enough to obtain the key from Beth (who had checked everyone in and held the room keys for them to make it easier when as everyone was arriving separately from different directions) for their mother's room for the 75th birthday celebration. Lynn had readied the room with a beautiful flowering plant, and chilled champagne and glasses. As they turned the first corner off the landing, they were all checking their keys for the numbers.

"No, down this way," Lynn instructed the others, leading the way down the first hall, then turning right again. At the corner of the hallway, Ann and Beth, daughter's number two and four, had the first room, number 214. They expectantly opened their door. Everyone peered in to see the larger room of a two-room shared-bath suite. Ann and Beth dropped off their suitcases and jackets onto their beds. The next room number 216, which shared the bath with Ann and Beth, was the room Jane, daughter number three, and her daughter, Christine, would share for the weekend. Everyone took a look-see at this room as well, for comparison's sake. The third room number 218 down this last

17

hallway would be Jane's other daughter, Leigh's, and beyond that one Lynn's room number 220, then 'birthday girl' Wren's room number 222 at the end of the hallway.

"How terrific -- we have the whole hall! All our rooms have a view out to the forest, and without any rooms on the opposite inside wall -- just windows overlooking the interior courtyard -- we have the run of the place to ourselves! Won't matter if we make a little noise!" Ann said.

"I booked it that way on purpose," Beth said, brushing her dark blonde hair back behind her ears.

"Excellent planning, now that we see the place," Jane agreed.

"I would have liked the rooms on the third floor, but there weren't enough beds up there. And," Beth added coyly, "that's where Pearl, the resident ghost, hangs about."

"Okay, I have that coming," Ann said. "You all know I hear things, see things. I can't help it. I just like to think of myself as 'receptive' to that other realm."

Wren smiled to herself. Of all her daughters, Ann was the most sensitive, most in tune with the occasional sign or voice to be heard, like herself.

"Yeah, right, Aunt Ann," Leigh laughed, as she turned the key in her door.

There was a rustling and a scuffling behind the women. They turned and found a man, medium height, medium build, heavy rimmed glasses, and undistinguished features in a rush, as he pushed his way through the group at the door now opened by Leigh. Once at the door, he grabbed the door, turned to them, and said, "Out, all of you out of my room!"

"Wait," Leigh said, her key still in the lock, "this is my room. Who are you?"

A Very Sisterly Murder

And with that, the man shut the door in all their faces. The women heard the deadbolt snapped locked on his side of the door. Beth quietly reached up and took Leigh's key from the lock.

"Whoa!" Jane said. "What's that all about?"

"I don't know, but come next door and we'll call downstairs to the desk and find out. Leigh, you still have all your things, right, you didn't leave anything in the room, did you?" Lynn asked.

"No, I only have my purse and backpack and they are right here. I never actually made it inside!"

"Okay, let's all go to next door to Lynn's room and get this settled," Wren, the group's matriarch suggested.

Just steps down the hallway, they entered Lynn's room. She picked up the phone and dialed the front desk.

"Hello? Yes, we seem to have a problem with the rooms up here. There's a man in one of our rooms -- yes -- yes, room 218, that's right," Lynn said. "Okay, right." and she hung up.

"Seems management will send someone right up to straighten this out. I can't imagine what this is all about," Lynn said.

Jane, Leigh's mom, was more than agitated, tossing her red curls a bit as she stuck her head back out the doorway and looked down the hall to the room next door.

"Whatever does this guy think he's doing?" she asked.

"Jeez!" Wren added.

In only a few minutes, a chambermaid was in the hallway, towels over arm, and keys in hand. She rapped her knuckles briskly against the solid oak door of room 218.

"Mr. Smith, are you in there? This is housekeeping, Mr. Smith," she said efficiently. The women huddled near Lynn's open door, some in the hallway, the more hesitant ones still in the room.

Shelly Young Bell

There was a rattling of inner security chains and deadbolt lock as Mr. Smith unlocked the door and opened it about five inches to the chambermaid.

"Yes?"

"I'm sorry, Mr. Smith, there seems to be some mix-up with the reservations for this room. We didn't know you'd be staying through the weekend -- "

"Why yes, I'm sure I told Mr. Brophy that I was staying the weekend for the class reunion. And since this bloody storm seems to be setting in rather violently. I won't be going to the cabin for the weekend. I'm sorry, but I'm staying the weekend." And with that he shut the door in the chambermaid's face.

She turned and looked at the women twenty feet down the hall. She was only the maid after all, what did they want from her? She smiled, and said, "I'll go downstairs and explain. Mr. Brophy will call up to your room in a couple of minutes with a solution." She turned, and was off down the hall. The women looked at each other.

"What just happened here?" Beth asked.

"I think I just lost my bed!" Leigh answered.

"Gee, I hope this doesn't upset you too much, you have to think about your sugar levels," Jane, her mother and always the nurse, said.

"Don't worry, ma. I haven't had to take any insulin for weeks, it seems to stay at a pretty safe level, unless I am under terrible stress. I don't count this as terrible stress! Heck, I can always drive home tonight -- it's only an hour."

"Don't be ridiculous," Lynn piped in. "They'll make good on our reservations. After all, Beth made them last July."

"That's right," Beth confirmed.

"The fact remains that he has possession of the room and we don't," Ann observed. "This could be sticky. And if the Inn *is* fully booked for

20

A Very Sisterly Murder

the weekend like they said downstairs at the desk, then we might have a problem."

"No problem," Wren said. "They can put a rollaway bed in my room."

"No! This was supposed to be your special weekend." Christine said.

"They can put the rollaway in my room," Lynn offered.

"Or better yet, in with Christine and me. We'll just be together all night anyway, talking and catching up on things," Jane decided.

"Oh, that will be good. Mr. Smith next door to you three. He'll be trying to sleep and you all will be up giggling and carrying on half the night. Seems a good and well-deserved solution." Ann added laughing, thinking to herself she was glad there was a whole bathroom with two doors between her and Beth's room and the room Jane, Christine and now Leigh would be sharing.

The phone rang in Lynn's room. She went in to answer it.

"Okay, yes, I think that's agreeable. And I'm sure you'll make some allowance on the bill for them since they are being so cooperative. Yes, okay then. Bring it up as soon as you can because we are all here and our rooms are all open," Lynn said, hanging up the phone. "Darn fools! How could they have messed up like that! We had our reservation in for so long, and this guy gets the room?"

"Well, possession *is* 90% of the law, so to speak," Ann said, "Why don't we go to mom's room and open that champagne and then we'll all be feeling better."

"Good idea," Wren added. It was after all her birthday, and had often said celebration is always preferable to anger and disappointment. The group headed down the hallway to Wren's room.

Beth, noticeably quieter than the others during all this exchange, still hung back in the interior of Lynn's room. She hadn't ventured out into the hall when the maid had come, hanging back out of sight. Now in

21

Wren's room, she fidgeted with the glasses and box of crackers for their pre-dinner party.

The rollaway bed arrived, and before the hour was out, it had been set up in Jane and Christine's room. It was a tight fit, but everyone seemed okay with the arrangement. But of course, a couple of glasses of bubbly helped.

Further down the hall, right at the corner of the hallway on the side of the Inn facing the front, Bill Dancer lingered in the doorway of his own room, the door slightly ajar as he listened to the altercation down the hallway. He had heard the women laughing and carrying on as they passed his room. He had peeked out to see what the situation was, and realized it must be a family group that had reserved all the rooms down the last hallway. Bill hoped they wouldn't be too loud and disturbing as he preferred it somewhat quiet to do his writing.

Then he spied the one lady with the red hair. She was quiet a looker, he decided. Maybe the weekend promised more than just concentrating on his writing. He wondered where they were from. Maybe he'd get the chance to ask them later at dinner. He'd keep a look out for the group of them as they all went down to dinner.

Then, as he was standing there, door slightly ajar, musing over a chance romantic meeting, there was a scuffle, and a man barged in through the group of them and entered one of the rooms. Bill opened his door wide open, felt to be sure his gun was still in the holster under his left shoulder, and was about to go to their aid, but saw there was no immediate need to do so. He didn't know what was going on, but it seemed a little strange. The dark-haired woman bristled and seemed ready to reach out and grab the intruder by the neck. The blond took two steps backward until she was against the window overlooking the courtyard two stories below them, immobile as she watched the man take possession of the room. The oldest woman, who was shorter than the others, craned her neck to see what was going on in the throng of

A Very Sisterly Murder

people. The two youngest girls were affronted by the man's hissing remarks to them, but stood their ground. The redhead attempted to jibe back at him but was cut off by his slamming the door in their faces. The other one, which Bill had seen earlier with the older lady and the redhead, was not in sight. He hoped she was not accidentally locked in the room with the man. Bill was ready to jump in and intercede if it were needed. The women all went in the room at the end of the hall, and the situation seemed to be over. Bill closed the door and flipped the privacy latch. Carefully he took his suit jacket off, and hung it in the wardrobe; he took his revolver out of the shoulder holster and after checking the safety was on, Bill slid it into the drawer of the nightstand. Something about the whole thing didn't set right on his 'detective nerves'. He'd have to give it some thought. There was something, something . . . something that seemed amiss.

Chapter 6

Beth was unusually quiet while she and Ann changed for dinner. Ann wasn't sure if perhaps it was the long drive that Beth had had, the incident with Leigh's room, or the impending storm that might strand them here at the Inn longer than they had planned. The wind was already whipping the trees. The rain beat at the windows more steadily and with larger drops than even a half hour before. Ann had only come a little two hours, but even so hadn't really been aware the weather was going to get this bad. Just an October rainstorm was what she expected. The maid had brought them all matches and candles in hurricane lamp holders, just in case the electric went down, with the explanation that because the Inn was up on a hill in the forest, it was subject to frequent power failures as falling tree branches took down the power lines coming up the long gravel road to the Inn.

Ann pulled on her stockings and her black dress shoes. No jeans and sneakers in the 1776 Restaurant for their mom's seventy-fifth birthday dinner.

"Beth, you want to use my cell phone to call the boys at home?" Ann asked.

A Very Sisterly Murder

"No. Thanks. I have my cell, but I told them I'd only call if there was a problem. We have three phones that share the minutes, so I hate to use up any minutes just to chat."

"Noted that," Ann agreed, as voices and laughter resounded in the hallway outside their room.

"Guess some of them are already headed downstairs. I think there is a bar, but I didn't see it when we came in. Maybe that's where they are headed."

"I don't know, with all that champagne we just drank?

"You are probably right. Maybe they are just anxious to see what's on the menu. We're five o'clock supper eaters at our house. Not full dinner at seven thirty. I'm starved already, and I still have another hour to wait." Ann said.

"Why don't you go on down, and I'll join you shortly. I seem to be taking longer than normal, and still need my turn in the communal bathroom," Beth said.

"Okay, here's the room key. You need it to lock the room from the outside. Meet you downstairs in the lobby area. If you don't see us, follow the trail to the nearest bowl of peanuts or crackers!" Ann said, getting up from the bed with her purse, and leaving. Quietly closing the door behind her, she paused on the hall side of the door, listening. What was with Beth? Was it just being away from the husband and the two boys, or perhaps she wasn't feeling well and didn't want to discuss it. There was no sound from inside the room. Nothing giving any indication of a problem. Nothing. But something was up, Ann knew it, her cop instincts activating. Ann turned and headed down the hallway towards what promised to be an excellent and fun meal.

When Ann reached the lobby, Lynn, Wren, Jane, Christine and Leigh were all there, huddled around a wonderfully roaring fire in the walk-in fireplace. They were studying the inscription under a painting of Mr. Johnson that hung over the fireplace.

25

"David Johnson. Made his fortune mining garnets that were discovered here in the 1850's. Built this Inn on the site and lived here the rest of his life as a 'guest'," Lynn said. The others studied the distinguished gentleman in the portrait.

"Beth coming?" Wren asked.

"Yeah, she'll be right along," said Ann.

"Our table is still occupied and won't be ready earlier than our reservation time," Lynn explained, rejoining the group having spoken with the maître d'.

"No problem. I've got to scope out the lay of the land anyway. Might as well do it right now," answered Ann. She took note of the nice sized lobby, old Victorian furniture grouped in front of the fireplace. There was an old organ on an adjoining wall. And shelves of old soup tureens. She read all the little explanatory note cards with each one. There was a bookcase with souvenir coffee mugs, beer glasses, chocolate bars and postcards. The hallway that led toward the back of the building gave way to the Café, where breakfast would be served in the morning, and then Pearl's, the small and dark bar. Pearl's -- perhaps the jewel, perhaps named after the wife of Mr. David Johnson? Ann peered in, not seeing much except a couple of people lifting glasses of their favorite adult beverage to their thirsty lips. One man, an especially nice-looking man, met her eyes, and then seemed to look past her as if looking for someone. She thought she had seen him before, but she could not place him. Then she turned and walked back towards the main part of the lobby to sit and wait for their table to be ready.

When they were finally led into the 1776 Restaurant, they were given the largest table and all sat without incident. Indeed, all the other tables were taken, mostly twos and fours. Ann noticed that the nice-looking gentleman from the bar now sat at a table very near to them. He was alone. The table was set only for one. And he had his eyes locked on Jane. Amused, Ann turned back to her menu.

A Very Sisterly Murder

Once the waitress came and took their orders for onion soup, house salads, and a variety of fish and beef entrees, Leigh said, "I don't see the man who took my room here tonight."

"Maybe he takes his dinner in his room," Wren offered.

"Maybe he is afraid that if he comes out, you'll rush in!" Christine laughed.

"Maybe, he already ate at an earlier time and we just didn't notice him coming and going off our hallway," Jane said.

"Look here, on the back of the wine list, it tells the story of the Mystery of Johnson's Garnets. Seems that Johnson had made a fortune in garnets and legend has it that the treasure is hidden here somewhere in the Inn. That would be something to find, wouldn't it? His wife, Pearl, became ill and died young while they were living in their third-floor apartment – explains the ghost stories," Lynn said, studying the back of the wine list.

"I think it's just an advertising gimmick. A fortune in garnets would have long ago been ferreted out and found. Can you imagine how many people have looked for it over the years?" Beth said.

"I agree with Beth -- just a publicity thing. No garnets. Not worth getting our juices flowing over. Besides, we don't have access to any of the really great hiding places in the Inn," Ann said.

Lynn pulled out her camera and laid it on the table.

"Maybe we could ask the waitress to take a group shot of us all together for mom's birthday."

"Good idea," Jane said. They all looked around for their waitress, who was busy with a table at the far end of the room.

The single man at the next table, obviously overhearing their animated conversation, rose and approached their table.

Bill Dancer addressed Lynn, who held the camera, "Allow me to take your photo. I would be happy to."

Shelly Young Bell

"Oh, thank you so much. We were going to ask the waitress, but she seems to be busy right now," Lynn said., handing him the camera. "It's your basic point and shoot camera. Here is the shutter. Take two or three shots if you will, so we can be sure we get a good one."

"Yes, of course," Bill answered. He stepped back quite away to be sure he had all the smiling women in the shot, then quickly took three shots. Returning the camera to Lynn, he introduced himself.

"I'm Bill Dancer. My room is not far from your rooms. I heard the altercation you had with that gentleman in the young lady's room this afternoon. I hope it all worked out okay for you?"

"Well, they brought up a roll-a-way bed and we'll squeeze together. No hardship, but a bit annoying," Lynn said.

Bill looked at Jane, "I hope you all are having a wonderful weekend here. Perhaps you'd all join me for a drink in Pearl's Bar later, if you'd like."

There was an awkward silence for a few seconds. Then Jane, whose eyes had met his and had understood his invitation said, "Well, perhaps if we happen to see you there later, we'd be glad to have a drink with you."

Wren's eyes twinkled and she added, "Since I am the birthday girl, I guess I'm entitled to a little drink this evening."

His eyes drifted back to Jane, who down cast her eyes in embarrassment. Bill gave a bit of a heel clicking, head bowing salute to the ladies, returned to his table to finish his coffee, and then just a few minutes later left the dining room.

"Well, he certainly is one pleasant man, much in opposition to that man up on our floor! A bit young," Wren observed, directing this statement in Jane's direction, "but very pleasant. Can't wait to see this infamous bar named after its infamous ghost!"

Chapter 7

Bill Dancer took his tie off and dropped it over the back of the arm chair in his room. The wind, fierce in the darkness, perhaps fiercer because of the darkness, pounded the old leaded window. He could see the curtains move ever so slightly as the outside storm wormed through the old window frame and breathed against the old velvet curtains. Was it Cathy reaching for Heathcliff in the night, far away on Wuthering Heights?

Stop! he told himself. He had to get his act together before he let his mind start to wander tonight. After all, it was no time to let his guard down. He hoped to keep his passion for writing to himself. Luckily the ladies had not asked him what he did for a living, or what his hobbies were. They were all happy to chatter on about their own weekend plans. Of course, he could have told them he was a detective, newly hired by the Philadelphia police force. That he was headed there to take up his new position on Monday morning. But he hoped to leave his whole life behind him this weekend and concentrate solely on writing.

He stepped over to the bed where he had laid his things carefully out on the matelassé bed cover – bathroom kit, fresh and folded socks, boxers and undershirts that smelled of the lime scented drawer paper

Shelly Young Bell

he used in his dresser at home. The scent was so much more noticeable here, in this old room.

Bill looked at the rest of his things that he had considered perfect for his country weekend, newly purchased for the weekend and for his new life in Philadelphia, still neatly laid out on the bed as he hung up the sport coat he had worn to dinner: two clean starched white shirts, two cashmere sweaters, two ties in appropriately subdued tones, and a pair of plaid pajamas for his private self, his new leather portfolio. He fluctuated between wanting to put his things away in the drawers of the dresser cum desk opposite the bed and sitting down to write immediately. The paper, the pen, the words called to him. He was itchy to get back to his story.

He mused over his first sight of her, the redhead. He knew there was something wonderful about her the minute he laid eyes on her across that room earlier. Out of the storm and the night and the cold he had entered into the warmth and fire of that gathering. He knew it hadn't been the brisk walk down the long hallways and the flight of stairs that had left him breathless. Heck, he was in better shape now than he had been ten years ago at the Police Academy. No, it was seeing her standing there, in her dark blue dress and simple strand of pearls, in the fire glow -- that is what had left him mute. A vision! Even now, after so short a period of time, and only the briefest of shared words – was he to believe what his heart was telling him? It was all that mattered right at this moment. Not even the unwelcome presence of all her family was going to cloud this new light in his soul.

He set up the desk with his portfolio, notepads, and pens. He sat in the little desk chair, switched on his brass table lamp, opened his leather portfolio and wielded pen to paper like the unbeliever in writer's block that he was. Bill Dancer played at writing his hardboiled detective and love interests as if it were *himself* living the adventure. He propped his stocking feet up on the radiator, and read the words he had written

A Very Sisterly Murder

earlier in the day back to himself out loud. Bill Dancer saw no humor in the scene he played out alone in his room. Reading his writing to the air, rapt in his own imaginings, it was all seriousness to him.

Bill could hold the words back no longer. The wind gusted and rattled his window against its frame. The lights flickered momentarily, but Bill Dancer did not notice. The sounds of the wind moaning in the treetops echoed down the hallways, the occasional door closing down the hall, laughing voices as some descended the grand staircase all disappeared from his consciousness. Bill picked up his pen and swiveled around in the chair so he was sitting upright at the desk. He was gone. Gone to a place of tinkling temple bells, rickshaws on the cobblestones, and a sea of voices he found unintelligible.

Interlude

Who knows how this thing they call love works? To be convinced late in life that it does indeed work at all was a great revelation. I was sitting in the bar at the Shangri-La Hotel in Hong Kong late on the most magnificent afternoon God had ever created on this planet.

I drank deep from my G & T with double lime, studying the skyline inclining up the mountains across the bay, the buildings truly alabaster in the sunlight, palms blowing in the breeze, heavy water traffic racing back and forth in the harbor — Chinese junks, cruise ships, freighters. Sensational, I thought. How could this moment ever be improved upon? I'd memorize it – for recalling during those mediocre days and weeks through which I usually only "existed".

I hadn't anticipated the scent of Chanel No.5 and a brief glimpse of navy chiffon . . . But there she was, so close, yet separated from me only by her own ignorance of my presence. I stood as she entered the bar; she was looking for someone or something. Funny, I knew it wasn't me, but somehow, I wasn't going to let that stand in my way. As she walked past me, I spoke.

A Very Sisterly Murder

"Hello, miss. Maybe I can help you?"

She threw me a glance, looked me up and down, her red hair shimmery against the navy dress.

"No, I don't think so," she answered, without smiling, without caring. She kept right on walking, turned a corner and was gone from view. Just that one moment was like a double shot of Russian vodka. It seared going down, but left its warm presence in every part of my body and soul.

Chapter 8

Maybe it was the champagne they had before dinner, or maybe it was the glass of port Beth had bought for her after dinner in Pearl's Bar with Mr. Dancer and the others, but Ann was definitely feeling the worse for it. It was unusual because Ann could handle a few drinks with no problem. Two drinks spaced hours apart should not have any effect on her. Maybe the buffalo tenderloin she had for dinner was a bit off and that was the explanation. But there was a definitely a feeling she couldn't explain. Maybe it was just too much excitement, too many things creeping back into her mind from the dark crevices of her past. Places and people that she had tried to forget over the years. And of course, her new worry – her eyes.

She wasn't sure, but earlier, when that man, Mr. Smith, had barged through them and into Leigh's room, she thought she recognized him. The way he moved, the type of glasses he wore . . . But perhaps she was wrong. It was hard to explain the feeling. Was he someone she knew? She couldn't put the face with the name. She knew no "Mr. Smith" but there was something about him that reminded her of one Mr. *Porter* from her college days.

A college professor she had had to fend off. Maybe it was him and she had lost the ability to imagine the Mr. Porter she had known as an

A Very Sisterly Murder

undergraduate as this Mr. Smith that she had seen for only a minute, if that long. His voice? Ann tried hard to recall Professor Porter's lecturing voice and his private voice when she'd be alone with him in his office reviewing her independent study project. No, she really couldn't be sure the two were the same. She tried calculating in her head how old he'd be now, twenty years later – 60? 70 perhaps? Could it have been him, under a different name? Why would he be using a different name? Why should he be here if it was? No, she must be mistaken, but it had given her a bit of a jolt there in the hallway that afternoon, a memory, long suppressed, rising up sharply from the dim past.

Beth was in their room, laying out her things for bed.

"You okay?" she asked Ann.

"Yeah, just feeling a bit off. I think it must have been the buffalo steak. Trying it sounded like a good idea when Lynn ordered it, but now I think it's making me feel weird."

"Go to bed. There will be a full hot breakfast in the morning, and you'll feel more yourself then."

"You're right, I'm sure. I just have to wait my turn in the bathroom. The girls out yet?"

"I think it's free, let me check." Beth walked across the well-worn oriental rug to the door to the joint bathroom. She tapped quietly on the door. No one answered.

"It's free."

Ann got up, dragging her flannel nightgown with her. No need to have brought anything pretty or less than functional for a trip with mother, sisters and nieces, she had decided when she packed her bag the night before. After Ann came out from the bathroom and had gotten into bed, Beth reached over and turned off Ann's light.

"We better get some shut eye if we're to be rested for the big day of shopping, antiquing and looking at quilts tomorrow. Go to sleep," was all Beth said.

Ann's eyes were already so heavy with sleep she was glad Beth didn't want to girl talk the night away like she was sure Jane and the nieces were doing in the room next door. *If* Jane had managed to leave Pearl's and Mr. Dancer, and return to her room. This man could prove too much of a distraction to the group this weekend. And just about at the point when Ann was trying to remember if he had told them why he was at the Inn this weekend, she was asleep.

Beth smiled to herself, got back out of bed to fetch a book and a small flashlight from her suitcase, and tried to read while the wind howled around the corner their room was on, rattling windows on both outside walls. The book she needed now, the flashlight she would need later. The lights flickered off and then back on. She reached over and lit the candle on their nightstand, just in case. She was glad she was not out in the storm, but safe and warm here at the Inn. This weekend would help relieve some of the tensions in her life, and in the lives of these family members around her. But it wasn't quite time yet. She looked at her travel alarm. Ten-twenty. She'd read for a while then check on Mr. Smith when Ann was so sound asleep, she'd not hear Beth leaving the room.

Down the hallway, Jane, Leigh and Christine had retired to their 'girl sleepover' room with the roll-away bed and clothes laying on every surface. Jane was glad her two daughters were here with her. Now that they were grown, it was hard to balance the desire to protect them and yet let them live their own free and young lives. She knew how much could go wrong. She was the one living with the illness that she wouldn't, or couldn't, talk about. She wouldn't let that thought cloud this weekend of fun with Leigh and Christine. This weekend would be a healing experience, at least emotionally. She was sure of it. When

A Very Sisterly Murder

Beth had suggested the weekend at the Inn, she had known she should be part of the plans. That she definitely *would* be part of the plans. And so now it was about mothers and daughters and sisters. The present and the future.

Two rooms further down the hall, Lynn ran a hot bath, setting big white fluffy hotel towels within easy reach. The lights went out, then right back on again. She poured a bottle of scented bath oil under the running water. Then she went to the dresser near the door and lit the candle that the maid had brought earlier. The lights seemed like they definitely would go out during the night, and if they did, Lynn knew that a naked woman in a bathtub was too much temptation for the gods to pass over. The lights would definitely go out the minute she dropped her robe and stepped into the steaming aromatic water. She carried the candle into the bathroom and set it on the back of the toilet. A little unwinding was needed.

Lynn had seen him, that man. He tried to shield his face from her as he pressed through the girls and took possession of the room, but he could not disguise himself from her. She knew him. And she hoped he recognized *her*. Give him a fright to know she was there at the Inn. It would serve him right. A hot soak, then she'd be dressed and ready in case Beth needed her help later.

In the end room on the hallway, Wren sat on the wicker chair that was in her sitting area. She was so pleased with the surprise birthday weekend. She had not expected Lynn to come from Buffalo, NY, nor Leigh from York, PA. She had thought it was a trip to hear Robin, Ann's daughter, sing with her school choir. But that turned out to be a ruse, just the means to get her into the van for the four hour drive down from upstate New York. Now she was tired, it had been a long, long day. The room was lovely, Lynn had arranged for a flowering plant which graced her nightstand, complimenting the overall floral motif of the room. The floral bedcovers and rug ran towards a Laura Ashley theme, but she thought perhaps it was more original than the 1980's craze over the British designer.

Wren wondered how they would all get along together for forty-eight hours. Her daughters had grown into women so different from each other, often at odds with each other. Tonight, they all seemed happy to be all together, but still Wren sensed an impending storm. And not just the storm wailing outside. Something was brewing, she could sense it, as she had often sensed things well before they happened. But she knew there was nothing she should do about it tonight.

Wren could tell by her daughters' reactions to this Mr. Smith that more was going on this weekend than champagne, birthday cake and quilts. Wren cared more for her family so very much, so she decided that whatever came, she'd be part of it and then keep her mouth shut to the grave. There were already too many things about this weekend for her to think it was all just coincidence. Sometimes her family called her fanciful – that she read too many books and imagined too many wild things, but she was sure that tonight and this weekend trip were much more than just a birthday celebration.

She opened her suitcase and took out her nightgown. The lights went out. She waited twenty seconds, but the lights did not come back on. She slowly felt her way over to the dresser a few feet away and there found the little box of matches and the candle in the pewter holder that the maid had delivered during their pre-dinner cocktail party in her room. She struck a match, the sulfur fumes rising to her nose and eyes. She lit the candle and was glad the power had not gone out during her birthday dinner party. She moved the candle to her nightstand, and getting into bed under the duvet, she let the candle shed its light on her tiny notebook where she jotted down thoughts and impressions of the day, of the Inn, and of her suspicions.

In the middle room along the hallway, Mr. Smith quietly paced back and forth the length of his small room. His possessions around him, he debated leaving the Inn at that very moment. He could pack and leave, giving some excuse about a phone call from a sick family member. He would disappear for the weekend like he normally did, and then resume his life on Monday as tenant of this room and sales person out in his territory. Part of him screamed to be gone from this place, but the other part of him desperately needed to stay and find out why they were here. How had they found him? What did they want?

It was almost more than he could bear, the suddenness of it. Ann was here after all these years. So near! How was it possible? He'd had no dinner, too afraid to leave the room and encounter them in the hallway again. He decided that he'd go down to the kitchen later for something to eat after everyone was in bed and the Inn was quiet. He would need to eat something before he could take his medicine. The bar would be open until two in the morning, so the kitchen should be open until then as well, at least for bar food.

How would he be able to attend his high school reunion the next night? Would he be able to work up enough nerve to come out of his room at all this weekend? He paced back and forth debating these things with himself. The lights flickered on and off several times, but Mr. Smith didn't seem to notice. He didn't pause to light his candle against the inevitable darkness. He just paced back and forth.

Chapter 9

Ann opened her eyes, her heart racing. She had heard a scream. She heard nothing now. Perhaps she had dreamt it. Perhaps it was the ghost of Pearl, a real and ghostly presence. She didn't dare move, didn't dare roll over to see if Beth was awake or asleep in the next bed. Slowly her senses started to come back to her. She forced herself to breathe more normally. What she thought was terror blinding her, was not. Her eyes adjusted a little better and she could see the travel alarm on the nightstand, but there didn't seem to be any other light anywhere. No light in the bathroom. No light from outside. No light shining under the door from the hallway. The power must have gone out. The storm raged on outside the Inn, the wind pelting heavy rain against the windows and the thunder seemed to roll on uninterrupted.

Slowly, Ann got out of bed, wrapping her robe around her. She lifted the room key off the nightstand, and went to the door. Silently, slowly she turned the deadbolt, hoping not to alert anyone. She opened the door a crack, saw absolutely nothing in the pitch black. She could hear nothing but the wind and rain and thunder. Suddenly there was lightning, and a tearing crack of thunder of such magnitude that surely no one slept through it. But still, no one appeared in the hall. Having forgotten to put on her glasses, she would not to be able to see anything

A Very Sisterly Murder

too clearly should there be the opportunity. She slipped out the door, just pulling it shut quietly behind her. No one would bust in on Beth at this time of night. She would just walk down the hall to listen at her mother's door to make sure nothing was awry. Ann kept her fingers on the wall to her left, counting doorways in the darkness. Ten steps down the hallway, past Jane's room. All quiet. Another ten steps down the hall, past Mr. Smith's room. All quiet. Ten more steps. Lynn's room was quiet. Then to her mother's room. Very quiet. Another crashing streak of lightening lit up the hallway from the windows facing the courtyard.

And there he was. A man at the end of the hall in the doorway that led down the back stairs to the kitchen and banquet area. Ann could have turned and run. She might have made it back to her room, but probably not. She decided to fight if it came to that. She hoped it would not. The man had heard her soft barefoot steps on the carpet and turned towards her.

"So, you've come," Mr. Smith/Porter said.

"It *is* you. I wasn't sure until just now. Here we are -- like before. Alone in the dark. With the devil," Ann said quietly, more in control of herself now that she was actively dealing with the situation and not just imagining it. She remembered an earlier time with a professor and an impressionable co-ed alone in a dark classroom building late one night. Professor Porter pressuring her to confront her deepest fears in the darkness of an unlit hallway. Of course, what he had wanted at the time was for her to succumb to his self-imagined charms. All this talk of facing fears was tommyrot. Ann knew she had beaten him and had escaped his clutches years ago, but here she was again alone in the dark with him.

Ann couldn't see his face very well in the dark, but it was as if she could sense the smile on his face. They say you can hear a smile in someone's voice. So, she waited for his reply, to hear it in his reply.

41

"Always the joker, you were," he said. And yes, he was smiling she decided. Another small burst of lightning and she could see he was moving closer to her. She would stand her ground.

"You didn't scare me all those years ago, on the third floor of McCallum Hall, playing at this 'worst fear' nonsense. You don't scare me now," she said, hoping her voice sounded more confident than she felt.

"Why have you come? What do you want? Is *she* here, too? I want to see her!"

"Nothing. We don't want anything. We came for my mother's birthday. You are paranoid. And *she* is not here. You'll never see her. She is *not* yours. I explained that ten years ago and I will keep explaining it if I have to. The timing is all wrong for her to be yours."

"I don't believe you. You ran off and a year later you returned with a baby. I knew that you – you weren't the type to just give yourself too freely, not easily. Lord knows how long I worked on you – she *has* to be mine!"

"No and Never! And I owe you no explanations – so stop asking. You are the mistake I will always regret. I have asked myself the last ten years how I could have been so short-sighted and stupid to have become involved with you. You offered nothing but control and jealousy. When I leave here Sunday, I will never see you again. Do you understand me? Do not attempt to pursue me or mine. I have a new name, a new life – out of your grasp forever!" Ann whispered at the man standing in the dark hallway, a whisper Ann was trying hard to keep from escalating into a shout.

"I don't believe you." He was inching closer to her. Ann feared he'd touch her, grasp her, hold her. She would refuse to let him, but she also did not want to show any weakness by retreating from him.

Suddenly, Ann could feel his breath on her neck. Too close! A wave of revulsion surged through her body. She wished she had more clothes

A Very Sisterly Murder

on, suddenly feeling vulnerable and unprotected, a teen again alone at college. She tried to control her own breathing, to make it normal, but was having a hard time.

Then, with the next flash of lightening, he was gone. Ann blinked, trying to focus her eyes, but without her glasses and in the dark, it was hopeless. The blood rushed to her ears and she heard nothing but a loud hum rising in her ears, blotting out even the rolling thunder outside.

No, no -- not now, she said to herself, fighting off the sensation of blacking out. No, no! Ann dropped to one knee and fought against it. It wasn't very long before she was able to breath normal. With renewed courage, she rose and turned her back to the far end of the corridor where her worst fear had stood, and walked swiftly back to her room. She needed to lie down. Once inside, she got into bed, robe and all. She'd deal with it all in the morning. Maybe she'd leave. Maybe she'd order room service for breakfast giving her time to think. That would keep her out of view until the family left for their day's outing. She would deal with the Saturday night dinner and Sunday morning brunch later. Ann hoped the whole situation would look brighter with the dawn.

Yes, she had been stupid as that young woman so many years ago and had let Mr. Porter manipulate her into believing it was okay to let him touch her, kiss her, take from her that which she'd never get back. She knew when that moment of intimacy was over, it was indeed *over*, never to happen again. She had expressed herself very clearly and frankly to him about ending any relationship he might fancy they had together, but Mr. Porter refused to agree it was over. He wrote her, called her, harassed her at every turn through the years after she was graduated from college; it continued on while she was at graduate school. When she could bear no more, Ann had pulled together her meager resources and flown to Scotland, on the pretense of finishing her Master's Dissertation there. Ann would be three thousand miles away from Mr. Porter's obsessive grasp. Ann had lived that year of her life in a daze of moors, stone country houses, and then acquiring a baby to call her own – Robin was not of her own flesh, but definitely was hers. Returning to the States, she had explained to her astonished family that Robin was a foundling and she had taken her in, she just couldn't leave the baby behind. As expected, her parents and sisters had been horrified that Ann had strapped herself, so young and unmarried, with a baby. But over the last ten years the details of that year abroad had become more like a dream than the drama that had actually played out in the mist of treeless hills, craggy peaks and blue-gray lochs. Looking back to those early months as a 'mom', Ann smiled in the dark. The best thing she ever did was to agree to take little Robin as her own.

She pulled the blanket up over her face so she wouldn't imagine seeing Mr. Porter's figure in the shadows cast by the lightning of the intensifying storm, and lay shaking until, eventually, drifting off to sleep.

Chapter 10

Even from under the blankets that she had pulled up over her head, Ann could hear the ringing of an alarm clock. Only it was not hers. Or Beth's. She pulled the blanket down off her head and raised her head up a bit to listen with both ears. Definitely an alarm clock. But down the hall a bit. The seconds ran into minutes and still the alarm continued on and on. It was daylight, so it had to be after six in the morning. The thunder and lightning had mercifully ended even though the wind continued. Someone obviously had forgotten to turn off their alarm when they got into the shower. Or something to that effect.

Ann rolled over. Beth was still in bed, but Ann couldn't tell if she were asleep or not. As the alarm went on and on, there was no chance of getting back to sleep. She reached for her glasses on the nightstand, then twisted her travel alarm clock around towards her so she could see that it was only six-fifteen. Too early for the Café to be open and serving coffee. Ann got up and headed for the bathroom. First to be in and out of the shared bathroom to use the shower couldn't hurt.

When she came out, Beth was up, sitting on the edge of the bed.

"Do you hear that alarm?"

"Yeah, woke me up. Thought it was mine."

Shelly Young Bell

"It's still going on. Someone ought to call the front desk and complain."

"Hopefully someone already has. I'd hate to be right next door to it," Ann said, getting her Saturday-Looking-At-Quilts outfit on. She was lacing up the last sneaker as someone screamed in the hallway.

It was a scream like she had never heard. And a lot more real than the scream she dreamt, imagined, or *maybe* heard, last night. But she believed last night's scream had only been an omen of the terror to come. She knew that only she had heard it deep within herself. Ann looked at Beth and they both went for the door. Unlocking it, they cautiously stepped out into the hallway, as had all the other occupants on this wing of the Inn's second floor – except one.

Down the hallway stood one of the young maids standing in the open door to room 218, her hands clutching her throat, her white maid's dress shaking with uncontrollable trembling.

"He's dead!! Dead! I've never seen a dead man before! Never! He's dead!" the maid was saying over and over. Wren came up the hall in pajamas and robe belted around her. She grasped the shoulders of the maid and backed her away from the door. Lynn peered in to take a look.

"Well, he's not moving at any rate, and it explains the alarm not being turned off," she said.

Bill, up already and dressed for his day in pleated slacks, white shirt and soft blue cashmere sweater, strode forward with authority amid the women, some of them dressed for the day, some still in nightclothes and robes. He was not wearing his shoulder holster under his sweater so he had left the pistol in the nightstand drawer. He had not foreseen the potential need for it during his quiet day of writing at this country Inn.

"Stand back, stand back. Don't touch anything. Does anyone have their cell phone handy? The power is still out and we need to call 911."

A Very Sisterly Murder

Jane slipped back into her room and fetched a cell phone. Handing it to him she asked, "And what do you know about this?"

Bill Dancer looked at her with a brief look of disbelief, then remembered that he had never told them that he was a police detective.

"I'm a detective, a police detective. Just moving this weekend to Philadelphia to take up a new position with the police force there. Didn't mention it before because this weekend wasn't about what I do for a living. Last night, I just wanted to be myself, the unprofessional me. Now, everyone, step back. Go back to your rooms and wait. I'll call the local police and get someone up here. Probably he just died in the night. But we have to do this right. Okay? So, now, everyone back to your rooms."

"Do you think you could at least turn off that infernal racket?" Leigh asked.

"Yes, I suppose I could do that without jeopardizing anything," Bill said. He first dialed 911 on the cell phone.

"Hello, yes, this is William Dancer, staying up at the Garnet Inn. Yes, power's out here too . . . oh . . . okay, well, we have a body up here . . . no, no obviously foul play, but without a forensics team up here, I can't do too much. Me? Yes, well I'm a detective with the Philadelphia Police Force, just here for the weekend. How soon will it be okay to attempt crossing the creek over that old bridge? . . . Do you think it will be washed away? . . . Well, do something creative about getting over here and taking over this thing. Okay. Bye."

He handed the phone back to Jane, their hands lingering over the transfer. Not too obvious, Ann decided. Ann knew she was going to have to be very careful from this point on. Yes, definitely recusing herself from taking over – she had no jurisdiction here anyways – and had to be so careful not to let anything be known about last night or that she knew who Mr. Smith *really* was, or their past history. She didn't kill him, she didn't even know if he had been killed, so there was no

47

Shelly Young Bell

need to involve herself. And that Mr. William Dancer would be underfoot back in Philadelphia, starting next week. Care was needed here and now.

"Okay, you heard the man, back to our rooms. At least until coffee is brewing downstairs. Yes, there will be coffee -- gas stoves, commercial kitchens use gas," Ann assured them. Beth had been standing right behind her. Neither one had looked into Mr. Smith's room. Neither one was too anxious to witness the scene. They headed back to their rooms, Wren turning the maid over to Bill Dancer once he emerged from Mr. Smith's room having silenced the alarm clock. Bill sat the maid own in one of the chairs in the hallway to rest until he felt she could get downstairs by herself.

"If you need any help, just let me know," Wren said.

"Oh? Help? In what way exactly?" Bill asked, wondering what the septuagenarian would be able to contribute.

"Well, I study crime, in books and in movies, you know, and I have been taking observational notes since we arrived, so I might be able to shed some light on things. Just thought I'd offer," she said.

"Well, gee, thanks. But it's just probably that the old guy died in his sleep, and when the medical examiner gets here, if he ever gets up here today, I'm sure there won't be anything to 'solve', if you know what I mean," Bill said.

"And my daughter, Ann, she works for the Philadelphia Police Force, so be sure to ask her help, too."

"Okay, I'll do that." Bill took a harder look at Ann. She had failed to mention this fact over drinks last night, but then so had he failed to mention he worked for the police. Had he met her at his interview, he wondered? He couldn't be sure. But as he had taken charge and Ann seemed none too willing to help, he would continue. Ann only smiled at him, saying nothing.

A Very Sisterly Murder

Wren went down the hall to her room. The others quietly went to their rooms and the doors closed behind them. Lordy, Bill thought to himself, old ladies and middle-aged detectives jumping to his aid. Not at all the way things were done. And he didn't even know if there had been a crime committed.

There was no blood, no evidence of a struggle. The room was in good order. The door had been locked from the inside. The place had not been ransacked. But this guy just laid on the bed fully clothed, with his eyes open staring at the ceiling. A 'die in his sleep' type thing? Bill wasn't an expert on that. He'd have to wait until the medical examiner arrived.

Bill went next door to 216 and gently rapped on the door.

"Yes?"

"It's Bill Dancer. I was wondering if I could borrow one of you for an errand?"

The door opened, Jane was dressed and was running a brush through her red hair in front of the mirror over the dresser. Steady on, Bill, he told himself. Steady on.

"Sure," said one of the younger women, also dressed, who came forward to the open door.

"You are. . . ?"

"Christine. Christine Bishop."

"Okay, well, Christine, I would like you to go downstairs and get the Inn manager to come up here. I don't want to leave that room unattended. I want to be able to lock it up with an official witness to the whole process. I can't imagine where he is -- after all, someone has died in his Inn. Surely they must know downstairs that there was a problem."

"Only that the alarm clock was going off, and was way too loud. I got dressed quickly and went down to find someone to come and turn it off. First person I saw was the maid on the staircase already on her

49

Shelly Young Bell

way up here to see what the matter was. But I'll go down and fetch the Manager. House phones are out because the electric is off."

And with that she went down the hallway and around the bend to the staircase out of sight.

Fair enough, Bill told himself. But this was *not* how he had intended to spend his day. Maybe if he was really lucky, this would all be cleared up by lunch, the storm would end, the power would come back on, the bridge would get repaired, the ladies could have their Birthday Quilt Outing, and then he could get back to his writing.

Chapter 11

Before Ed Brophy, Inn Manager, arrived to witness the locking of the door, Bill Dancer had another cursory look around room 218. Nothing broken. No strewn-about clothing. With the end of his pen, Bill opened the desk drawer. Nothing but a Gideon's Bible, and some Inn letterhead and envelopes. The closet door was slightly ajar, so again with the end of his pen, Bill swung it open to have a quick look. Everything neat and tidy, hung up in order. Enough clothes for quite a few days. Not a weekend trip obviously. Dress shirts, sport coats, dress slacks. a couple of outdoor jackets, four pair of assorted shoes on the closet floor. On the shelf overhead, two suitcases, medium quality, well worn, well used. Bill moved on to the dresser. He didn't risk trying to pry open the drawers and he didn't touch the knobs as he'd disturb any fingerprints. On top of the Victorian piece was a set of combs and brushes, a stack of paperwork indicating he must be working for a textbook company in some capacity, and a couple of old volumes of W.B. Yeats poetry and his emergency candle, the wick still fresh and unlit, so Mr. Smith had not risen to light the candle when the electricity went out about 11:00 p.m. Bill reasoned the man must have been dead before he would have needed to light his candle.

Then he took a quick look into the small bathroom. Bill could make out towels hung up, fresh, unused since the maid had changed them yesterday, personal items setting on the shelf over the sink -- toothbrush, toothpaste, deodorant, floss, and bottles of pills, a used but empty glass.

Bill stepped into the bathroom, and with his elbow flipped the lights on. Stupid, he said to himself, the power is out. He'd have to wait to see what the prescriptions were in better light since the bathroom was an inside room with no window. One of them might indicate a possible cause of death. This Mr. Smith had not been a young man. It had been dark. Bill could envision it clearly – this old guy having some difficulty and needing to take medication. In the darkness of the storm, he mixes up the bottles or miscounts how many pills he has shaken into his hand.

Bill looked at Mr. Smith. Or what had been Mr. Smith. Maybe he just had a heart attack and laid down on the bed and died. Power was out, so he couldn't call downstairs for help. Yep, that was pretty much what must have happened. But the medical examiner would determine cause of death, not him, not a police detective without any local jurisdiction. Still, being alone with a body in the room was spooky. He had not yet gotten over that feeling. His work usually came after -- after the body had been removed, after the men in white had come and gone -- the slow methodical fact gathering, the piecing together of details, the eventual coming to a conclusion. But that wasn't the way it played out this time.

Tomorrow after teatime, he'd be out of here, on his way to the big city to his new job. The big city -- real crime, real adventure. No more backwater variety, Saturday night domestic dispute, drunk and disorderly, speeding through town type crime. Bill wanted real crime -- murders, espionage, terrorism, graft, corruption. He figured he'd work at that until he was burnt out, then he could return home to his family's farm to retire to putter and write. His eyes twinkled at the imagined

A Very Sisterly Murder

thoughts of Bill 'The Big City' Detective. But now, he just wanted Mr. Brophy to get up here, so they could lock the door, await the medical people to come and remove Mr. Smith, and he could get back to his writing.

Bill heard footsteps approaching in the hallway. He stepped out of the room into the hallway and met Mr. Brophy, already noticeably perspiring at the temples and nearly hand-wringing over the terrible, terrible misfortune of someone dying in his Inn. How was he to explain all this. Terrible, Terrible!

"You don't have to explain anything, Mr. Brophy. Just lock up the door so no one can get in until the medical examiner arrives. The key is in the keyhole where the maid had inserted it. Then take this poor maid downstairs with you and get her some strong, hot, sweet tea."

"I don't know how soon that will be. Phones are out, electric is out, bridge is out, for God's sake!" Mr. Brophy said, his voice rising to a new height of anxiety.

"Just lock the door and be calm. If I were you, I'd make sure there was coffee and breakfast for the rest of the guests. There will be talk. The staff knows obviously. Everyone on this floor knows. How many other people are there in the Inn this morning that probably don't already know?'

"Oh, thirty-six. But only if they are deaf and dumb. With all the commotion this morning, I can't imagine anyone slept through the screaming and carrying-on," Mr. Brophy said, turning the master key in the lock, then giving the door a vigorous shake to be sure it was securely locked. "It's locked, and it will stay locked. Oh, it's dreadful. A body. How will I explain all this?"

Bill watched Mr. Brophy pigeon walk quickly down the corridor and then turn out of sight around the corner. Glad to be rid of him, Bill started back to his room, when Jane popped out of her room.

"Mr. Dancer?"

53

Shelly Young Bell

"Yes?" Bill said turning to her.

"Phone for you," she said, holding out her cell phone to him.

"How -- "

"They must have taken my phone number down when we called 911 earlier. They want you."

"Hello, Bill Dancer here. Okay. Yes, I see, but . . . okay. No. It's okay. Really. Yes. Yes, but try to get someone up here. I don't care how swollen the stream is, and I don't care if the bridge might be swept away! Get a team up here." Bill handed the phone back to Jane. Her mouth twitched back and forth, the question poised there, but unasked. Bill knew what she wanted to know.

"I'll be talking to everyone soon. Just to get the facts down on paper before anyone forgets anything," Bill assured her and then he turned and went back to his room. He didn't have any of his work tools with him. No gloves, no special plastic zip bags, no anything. He looked around the room and decided on his new leather portfolio. He opened it up and took out his story, sliding it into the desk drawer out of sight, not confident enough to share even the fact that he did write, let alone share the actual story. Besides, it wasn't finished yet, he rationalized. With his portfolio and its now blank note pad and a pen, he left his room. He'd start at the far end of the hall and work back up towards his room. Then he'd be done with this until the local authorities arrived, and he could hand the body, the witness statements and the entire situation over to them.

Chapter 12

Bill Dancer knocked on the door at room 222. Wren opened the door. She was now dressed, and by the paperback in her hand and the afghan askew on the chair had obviously been reading a book by the window in the sitting alcove of her room. She had a nicer room than his, but then he had opted for a cheaper room for his weekend stay since all he meant to do was lose himself in the words in his head.

"I'm sorry to bother you, but the local police have asked that I take statements from everyone who witnessed the situation. This will get it out of the way and then everyone can be free to do whatever it was they had planned to do today."

"Come in then. But somehow, I doubt any of us will be going on about our normal business today, do you?" Wren asked. She led him over to the two wicker chairs set in the nook by the windows.

"Please start with your name and address, and then tell me your activities since six o'clock last night until this morning when the maid found Mr. Smith dead," Bill asked, making sure he gave her a wide enough window of time within which Mr. Smith had surely died.

After giving him her personal information Wren said, "You know very well that we were at dinner until nine o'clock, then we had a drink with you in Pearl's Bar until about ten o'clock or so. I came back up here to my room after that. It had been a long day for me and I tire more easily than my daughters sometimes realize. I changed into my nightclothes, wrote in my journal for a bit, then blew the candle out about eleven, and slept soundly until this morning when that alarm clock started ringing. It was very, very loud – loud enough to wake the dead. Oh! Sorry. Didn't mean that."

Bill ignored the 'dead' remark. He found it always better to ignore the awkward. He opened his portfolio and clicked open his pen. He wrote down her particulars. Noted to himself but did not put down on the paper that she didn't look the seventy-five years that she and her family were celebrating. Her dark hair, natural and untouched, made her look more like sixty. Not frail, and very aware for someone seventy-five. He ignored the feelings that she could have been an ally and not a suspect. Everyone had to be a suspect until proven otherwise, or until the fact was established that no crime had been committed.

"Did you know Mr. Smith?"

"Never laid eyes on him before."

"Tell me about why you and your family members are here and what happened yesterday, when you all arrived and came up to your rooms."

"You know what happened. You were there."

"Yes, but you have to state it in your own words, so I can put it down here on paper. Then you read it and sign it signifying that I wrote it down right. It will save a lot of trouble when the electric comes back on, and the medical examiner comes and takes Mr. Smith away."

"All right. We arrived. There was a bit of a 'surprise' in the lobby, like I hadn't been suspicious for the last three months. A weekend away, three days before my birthday? Well, it is a nice thought and I was having a good time until all this started. Well, anyway. We came upstairs, we have – had -- all the rooms along this whole hallway. Ann and Beth in the first room, Jane and Christine in the second room, then the disputed room Leigh was to have, then Lynn and me. When Leigh was going into her room -- I mean, they gave us a key and everything! -- this man, this Mr. Smith, came barging right through everyone, went into the room and told us it was his room and he wasn't giving it up. Next thing we knew the door was shut and locked. I haven't seen him since. Until, of course, this morning, when the maid opened the door to complain about the alarm clock."

"You didn't hear or see anything unusual through the evening or during the night?"

"No, like I said, I came back up, wrote a little, and went soundly to sleep."

Bill finished writing down her statement and had her sign it after she had read it.

"Okay then, I guess that will do. Thank you. Who's in this next room?"

"My eldest daughter, Lynn."

"Well, thank you again," Bill said. Wren got up to let him out. He took a dozen steps towards room 220 and knocked quietly on the door. The door opened quickly.

"Yes? Oh, it's you. Well, come in, let's get this over with."

Wren slowly closed the door behind him. She knew she had not given away anything she suspected. He hadn't even asked to see her notebook. Where was his head? Obviously *not* on his work. On daughter number three, perhaps? Wren hoped that was to their advantage. He hadn't noticed she didn't correctly answer his question about whether she knew Mr. Smith. True, she had never met him, but she knew *of* him. She wouldn't have wanted to know him. Not after the havoc he had wreaked on her daughters. She wouldn't have told this detective what she saw in Lynn's face yesterday when she confronted Mr. Smith, or the under-the-breath curse from Jane during their altercation. She wouldn't have given away why Beth had been so

57

reticent in the hallway, and then so quiet the rest of the evening. As for Ann, her lack of professional action in this situation had confirmed Wren's suspicions. No, Mr. Detective would have to find out for himself. Wren knew she had had no involvement in the death of Mr. Smith. She would involve herself no further. Just get past this and move on, she told herself. All their lives would be infinitely better.

Chapter 13

Lynn let Bill into her room. Smaller than his room, but in a way prettier. All white with violet accents, the color and the flower. There was only one chair, so he motioned for her to sit. He'd stand, balancing the portfolio on one arm while he wrote. This wouldn't take long.

"Name, address," he started again. When he had written it all down, he again asked the obvious, "Where were you between six o'clock last night and this morning when the maid discovered Mr. Smith's body?"

And he got the obvious "You darn well know where we were -- we were with you! At least until about ten-thirty. I don't really remember the time. I'm taking a little vacation this week-end, I'm not watching the clock all that carefully. Then we all came upstairs, and I took a hot bath and went to bed. Slept until that alarm clock got us all up so early. No sleeping in this morning. I could do with a nap right now, in fact!" She was acidy, but it had been a rough morning. He had seen people act in all sorts of ways in the face of a sudden death.

"Did you hear anything unusual during the night, or this morning?"

"No. Nothing. Slept soundly, until that blasted alarm clock!"

"I see. Okay, well, if you'll just sign this statement, I'll move along."

Lynn took the pen briskly from him and signed the piece of paper after a cursory look at it.

"It's a shame the guy died and all, but I don't see why all this is necessary."

"Nevertheless, I was asked to do this, so I am obliging. Thank you, miss. Now, I'll just be on my way. I only have a few more to do. Then we can have some breakfast and get on with our day."

Lynn rose from the chair, opened the door and let Bill walk quietly, unhurriedly, past room 218 with Mr. Smith still on the bed, and to room 216 where he knocked quietly and was let in.

Hmmph! She said to herself. A right cock-up for a detective! The guy next door is dead, and this detective doesn't even seem to care! What's his story? She would have loved to have been the one to ask Mr. Bill Dancer, Detective, the same questions he was asking, or was supposed to be asking, them. He *had no clue* what he was doing. Or was he just being wily? No, she decided, not wily, not coy, not the essence of the unassuming Peter Falk as Detective Columbo. He was too young to remember "Columbo" on TV. No, just green behind those sweet ears of his, and too distracted to see what was obvious. Just as well.

Yes, she knew Mr. Smith. But as Mr. Worthington Porter. *Dr.* Worthington Porter. He looked older and smaller than when he had threatened not to let the University's committee grant her the PhD. He had let her go through the three years of classes and research for her dissertation, but only then at the end did he have the nerve to tell her that he was fixing to make sure she was not granted the PhD. He wanted to get back at Ann, to punish Ann by punishing her sister from attaining what she had wanted most. He couldn't have Ann, so Lynn would never have the PhD! Simple revenge. Ha! Look who's laughing now. Lynn realized she was perversely glad to be here this weekend – to see the end of one Dr. Worthington Porter, a.k.a. Mr. Smith.

Chapter 14

It was even a much tighter fit in the room Jane, Leigh and Christine were sharing. It was the smaller of the two rooms that shared a bathroom. Nice, but tight with the extra rollaway bed and the jumble the three women had made of their clothes, packages, and suitcases. Bill discretely took a seat on the edge of the bed closest to the door. He tried hard not to wonder if it were Jane's. He kept his eyes on his notepad, knowing full well these feelings were not those of a professional. He was losing his head over this girl, and now he could see it was clouding his interrogation techniques. But he pressed on; it was the only thing he could do.

"I'll start with Christine, then Leigh, then Jane. Give me your name and addresses. Then I'll just get your whereabouts between six last night and this morning when the maid found the body."

The girls each gave the same basic story he had heard before: dinner, drinks with him at Pearl's bar, upstairs to change for bed, then they talked for a while before falling off to sleep. None of them remembering exactly what time that would have been. It could have been as late as midnight, or it might have been earlier. Then the power had gone off and they lit their candle but they not sure when that was. They waited until Ann and Beth had used the bathroom before getting themselves ready for the night. So, it figured they turned in a bit later than the other women.

When asked if they had ever met Mr. Smith before the encounter in the hall yesterday afternoon, Jane had to admit that yes, she had met him once before. She knew if they did any background checks, they may turn up that Mr. Smith had crossed her path, under the name Mr. Smith, not his actual name. Her actions now could prove crucial to her sisters' plot. Jane tried to answer as naturally as she could, showing no alarm. She was a nurse, which Bill already had learned the previous evening, and Mr. Smith had once been in hospital where she worked, she believed. She remembered him slightly.

"What was he being treated for, do you remember?"

"It was five, maybe six years ago. So many patients between then and now. Let me think. Heart, I think. I am not really sure."

"Heart problems would certainly explain his sudden demise," Bill admitted, more to himself than to the others.

"It's all so dreadful. And with the storm and all, this hasn't turned out to be the weekend we all had hoped for," Jane added.

"Yes, well, maybe in a bit, after the medical team arrives and removes Mr. Smith, and the power comes back on, and you all have a hot meal downstairs, things will look brighter," Bill said, trying to comfort them -- Jane in particular as he could see this situation was distressing her.

"Yes, perhaps," Jane concluded. She rose to show him the door. She knew the interview was over. She quickly added her signature to Christine's and Leigh's on his notepad. He smiled at her, and she tried her best to not notice. How could she notice? What good would it do her? She'd be heading home to Baltimore, two hours away from Bill Dancer who would be in Philadelphia starting Monday. No long-distance relationship for her.

A Very Sisterly Murder

Bill Dancer left their room and Jane closed the door behind him. For good, she hoped. As far as she was concerned this ordeal was over. Over for good.

She was surprised how easy it had been, not giving too much away when Bill started asking questions, but just enough to help convince Bill that it had probably been death by natural causes. Yes, she had been Mr. Smith's nurse some years ago. If the police did check for any reason, they'd find that it was longer than five or six years, but that could be just a casual bad remembering of the passing of time on her part. This Mr. Smith had turned on her one night, attacked her and stuck her with a used needle. Now she carried the burden of that infection forever. And the searing burning words Mr. Smith said to her all those years ago. "This will teach Ann; this will show her. You'll suffer like I suffer. Here, in my heart and soul." Mr. Smith had said to her. Unrequited love had driven him to seek the destruction of Ann's family. He had sought Jane out, found where she worked, exaggerated his heart problem to get admitted to her floor, then when Jane was alone in his room, he jabbed her with the needle from a hepatitis patient that he had secured earlier. And since then, she had lived a solitary life, fighting the infection, out of work on disability, because of this dreadful man and his obsession.

Jane couldn't have wished for an easier or more gratifying outcome. She had not figured in the investigating detective developing a crush on her. But that would go nowhere. It could not go anywhere. But his attention had been a pleasant diversion.

The girls patted her hand. They knew. She shared most things with them. They were her rocks, her anchors. It was all over now and there would be no need to talk about it. The less they talked about it, the safer they all would be, and the more normal Jane could feel her life was. Jane would try to focus on the good things and not her illness nor its cause. Today would be a long hard day, but soon it would be tomorrow.

Chapter 15

The door was already open to room 214. The two sisters had anticipated Bill's arrival, having heard the voices through the open door of Jane's room, and figuring their turn would be very soon. Ann and Beth were looking out the window as he tapped on the door and he entered the large room with two double beds. The wall the two beds were up against was the side wall to his room. But he had heard no noise from this room through the wall since they had all checked in late yesterday afternoon. This all added to his conclusion that no one had heard anything during the night. Nice solid walls. The wind howling all night. And he himself had heard nothing.

"Hello there," he said, so as to not startle them.

"Hello, come in," Ann said.

"Just a few questions, to put things in time perspective. Then the local police won't have to bother you."

"Sure," Beth said. "I think they must have risked coming across the bridge or something, because an ambulance just drove up to the main door of the Inn."

Bill smiled, relieved the end of this situation seemed at its end. "Then we'll make this quick. I'll want to be at Mr. Smith's room when the medical team goes in. If the medical team has arrived, the local

A Very Sisterly Murder

police must be with them. I need to get these witness statements finished and to them. Okay, give me your names and addresses, and a brief timeline of where you both were from six last night until this morning when the maid found the body."

"Getting tired of asking the same question?" Ann asked.

"What?" Bill asked, a bit taken off guard.

"Well, I figure you have asked that question quite a few times already this morning. And I bet you are getting some pretty boring answers, as we are mostly a pretty boring group."

"Yes, well, if I could just get your version of the events."

"Pretty simple really. Had dinner, then drinks with you, then up here to bed and a little reading while we waited for the noise next door to settle down. Nieces, you know, exuberant," Beth led off, having turned away from him, still half looking out the window with the floor length lace curtain pulled back with one finger.

"That's right," Ann added, "not much to help you out."

"Did you hear or see anything unusual during the night or early morning hours?"

Ann kept her eyes on the floor, waiting to see if Beth would give away her mid-night ramblings. But Beth just shrugged her shoulders and said they had both slept soundly through the night. Ann was a bit surprised, but kept her eyes downcast and her body language dead still. Why would Beth want to keep Ann's nighttime doings a secret? Did Beth think Ann had something to do with Mr. Smith's death! What a terrible thought! But maybe Beth had been so soundly asleep that she had not noticed Ann slipping out during the middle of the night. Ann originally thought she had dreamt the terrible encounter in the hallway, but when they got up this morning, she still had her robe on, and the room key was still in her pocket. She *had* been alone in the hallway with Mr. Smith during the night. She knew she should tell the detective, but what good would come of it? Nothing had happened that was

Shelly Young Bell

germane to the cause of death of Mr. Smith. There hadn't even been a scuffle. No one else had come or gone in that time. No one had even cracked open their door to see who was talking in the hallway.

Suddenly the overhead chandelier and bedside lamps flashed on. The power was back.

"Thank goodness," Bill Dancer said. It was a great relief. Now with the local police having arrived, the medical team here to take the body away, and now finally the electricity back on to power the hot water for showers and a good hearty breakfast downstairs, the day had started to look brighter. He smiled to himself. Yes, indeed, the day was looking brighter.

"Well, if you two will just sign this statement, I'll be out of your way."

The girls signed their names after a brief look at what he had written. They gave him the pen back and he was out the door, just as the Mr. Brophy with the master key, the paramedics and medical examiner were coming down the hallway.

"Here, let me show you the way," he said to the lead paramedic.

Chapter 16

Beth shut the door behind him. "Guess it's time for breakfast," she said.

"Guess it's time for some truth," Ann countered.

"You're a fine one for 'truth'. You weren't completely honest with that police officer, now were you?"

"No, I wasn't. I *was* in the hall last night, but there was nothing to report, and it would neither help solve nor foil the attempt to solve Mr. Smith's death."

"Convenient. But frankly I appreciate you did *not* tell him anything, actually. If you had, the police would never let up. Did we all know him, how did we know him, why are we all here if we all knew him -- "

"What do you mean 'we all knew him?' I knew him yes, years and years ago the bugger wouldn't take no for an answer and made my life generally quite difficult, but you and the others?"

"Not here, not now. It's over, that's all there is to it. Come on, the others will already be downstairs," Beth concluded. Beth steered Ann, still aghast with suspicions just surfacing, towards the door. When she swung it open, the rest of the family stood there. Mother and sisters and nieces, specters in the newly found hall lighting.

"Ready for breakfast?" Jane asked.

"Yes, I think we are," Beth answered. "If we can get Ann here moving *forward* and not backward."

"Ah, I see. Has she 'joined us', so to speak?" Lynn asked.

"Not exactly. Not yet anyhow. She thinks we have some explaining to do," Beth replied.

"Okay. Let's get it over with," Wren decided for the group and pushed them all into room 214, and firmly shut the door behind them, as the hallway was filling up with police and medical people.

"What's going on?" Ann wanted to know.

"He's dead, that's all that we need to know," Jane answered.

"No, you might as well tell her, though she'd be better off not knowing," Wren said.

"I think I'd be better off knowing than wondering, suspecting and imagining," Ann said.

"Okay, what do you suspect?" Beth asked.

"I think you killed him! But why?" Ann said, taking a step back away from them, making sure she was out of their grasp, physically as well as mentally.

"Go on," Wren said.

"I suspect you knew he'd be here and that is why we had to have this birthday getaway here, this weekend. I thought it was odd that no matter how reasonable it would have been to have the weekend closer to mom in upstate New York, Beth continually insisted it be here at the Garnet Inn. I suspect that for some reason I will never fathom, you or all of you had decided that Mr. Smith had to be done away with. I suspect that I was doped last night to put me out of action during the nighttime hours so you all could do your dirty deed. I suspect that Jane toyed with Bill Dancer yesterday and today to distract him and cloud the truth. I suspect that you all lied this morning when interviewed by Detective Dancer."

A Very Sisterly Murder

"Oh, and you didn't lie to Detective Dancer this morning?" Beth laughed.

"Well, it wasn't important to Mr. Smith's death, now was it?" Ann asked defensively.

"Was it, or wasn't it? How would we know? We weren't out there with you, were we? We just know you did manage to shake off the drug I mixed into your nightcap and roam around at a most inconvenient hour," Beth said.

"So then, did you kill him? Why?" Ann said in a tight horrified croak. Her sisters! Her *mother*!

"We all know how he hounded you after you rejected him at college. We all know how he would do anything to make you his, and when he couldn't, he tried to get to you through us. Yes, I know, we never let on. Why should we, then he would have succeeded in his plan to ruin your life by ruining our lives?" Beth said.

"I don't believe you."

"Believe it," Lynn said. "He managed to get on with his life, leave that college you went to, finish his doctorate and was teaching at Columbia when I was getting my doctorate. When Dr. Porter realized who I was and that I was so conveniently near, he must have come up with his plan to try to ruin your family. He was on the committee for my dissertation, and nearly was able to deny me the degree. But luckily the rest of the committee came to their senses, realized him for the obsessive madman he was, and overruled him. I got the Doctorate, and he moved on to torment Jane."

"Yes, apparently when he was thrust out of Columbia in disgrace for the way he handled the dissertation thing with Lynn, he changed his name to Mr. Smith and his job to selling textbooks. After some research he found me and was able to get himself admitted to the hospital where I was working," Jane continued. "I didn't know him from Adam. He was just a patient who needed meds and occasional monitoring during

69

Shelly Young Bell

my second shift. But he engineered making sure he was ready with a syringe he had swiped from a nearby trash bin. A needle used on a patient with hepatitis and he jabbed me with it. Yes, I know, that sounds rather melodramatic, doesn't it, but he was desperate to do as much damage to your family as he could. The damage was done. I have hepatitis now, will never be rid of it. He told me afterwards it was because he wanted to destroy you and those you loved, since you would never love him. I didn't share that with you, how could I? It would have made you miserable and not made the situation any better.

"He did a terrible thing to our mom," Leigh added, Christine nodding in agreement, "we had our chance to be sure that it didn't go any farther than it already has."

Beth took up the story. "Although he tried with Lynn and Jane to ruin their lives, he didn't totally succeed. But then he decided to start in on the next generation." Beth paused, letting the reality of that statement sink in before continuing. "After the incident in the hospital with Jane, he threatened Leigh and Christine, who were still young at the time, so Jane moved to Baltimore with her girls to escape him. Then he started in on my two boys. I wasn't going to put up with that. I know, I know, why not let the authorities take care of the matter? Right, like they even cared or believed us. They needed a crime to have been committed. They were not in the *prevention* of crime business. You ought to know that. The local police were of absolutely no help. So, what were we to do? I had to watch my boys like a hawk, making sure that man never came within striking distance of them. Then . . . "

"Then," Wren took over, "I had an unusual phone call. Someone, a man, looking to contact Robin," she paused waiting for Ann's reaction, her realization, before continuing. "I didn't tell him anything. I wouldn't give out any information on anyone without knowing who the caller was, and luckily the phone call seemed strange to me, so I put the man off. When I mentioned the call to Beth, she knew immediately what

A Very Sisterly Murder

was happening and filled me in. All these years I have had no idea all this was going on. Not until a couple of months ago when I got that phone call. And frankly once I knew all the facts, it was obvious something had to be done. I just didn't know it would be this weekend, until this morning."

"Mom!" Ann exclaimed.

"Oh, it wasn't mom's doing," Beth confessed, "but once she told me about the phone call, and we started piecing together what he might be up to next, we knew that it would never end. Until we ended it. So, I tracked him down, It's not hard with the internet and all. And what do you know, classmates.com proved more than helpful. I located him online, found out his class reunion was this weekend, at this Inn, and took a chance we could intercept him somehow. I never *dreamt* he'd basically hand himself over to us on a silver platter. So, we booked the rooms, not filling you in on the real reason for the weekend, but kept up the cover of the seventy-fifth birthday party. We didn't tell mom ahead what we had planned. Seemed better if she didn't know. And there you have it."

"But did you actually *kill* him?" Ann asked, needing to know, not wanting to know.

"In a word, maybe, probably. I knew you had left our room and confronted him in the hallway. I was listening. I heard him open the door at the far end of the hall and sneak downstairs to the kitchen. After you came back, I went out and knocked on his door. He wasn't there, and I still had the key that reception had given us for Leigh. I knew it was my moment of opportunity. From there it was simple to empty the medication for his heart out of the capsules, wash it down the sink, and place the empty capsules back into the bottle. At some point, he'd need that medication, and well, it wouldn't be of much help to him. But don't worry, my Detective sister, no fingerprints, I was careful. And this morning while that Mr. Bill Dancer was interviewing the others, I took

71

Shelly Young Bell

the opportunity to again use the key to his room which I still had, took the empty pills out of the bottle and flushed them down our toilet. It will appear he had run out of pills and couldn't call downstairs for help in the middle of the night. Too simple, really. When the medical examiner does the autopsy, if they decide to do one in these backwoods, they'll find his heart medication didn't help him much, or maybe he didn't have enough of it. Or maybe it was natural causes. He wasn't a young man after all. Maybe it was suicide. He has no family, he has no one close. The staff here didn't care about him, as he was just a paying guest. I checked it all out ahead. Although he had his family's cabin in the woods for weekends, he lived here most weekdays while he was out selling textbooks. Stripped of his teaching credentials after the fiasco he made of things with Lynn, he was reduced after all these years to being a second-rate salesman in a second-rate territory. You really humiliated him without even knowing about it."

There was a long, uncomfortable silence.

"Now what?" Ann asked.

"Now, it's time for hot coffee and breakfast," Wren answered. "It's over. For good. None of us will *ever* speak of this again. He was a monster. Never forget that. He can't touch anyone in our family anymore. And don't pass judgement on the rest of them. They did it more for you and for Robin than themselves. Come on, I'm ready for coffee, it's been a hell of a long night and morning already."

Ann wasn't sure what to say. Her head was filled with the vision of Mr. Smith somehow getting an opportunity to hurt her darling, Robin. She had feared that possibility for years, unconsciously looking over her shoulder, afraid he'd be there eventually. There would be feelings of guilt – that she was involved in this and covering it up, that Mr. Porter had hurt those she loved most. Ann knew she'd have to deal with that and carry on. But now, within the midst of her sisters, mother and nieces, she made the only choice she could. She would be one of them, one of these sisters in crime.

Shelly Young Bell

Chapter 17

Bill Dancer was glad to give over this case to the local police. An old guy had died in his room alone with no evidence of anything to the contrary. He had lain down on the bed and died -- that is what they would find out. Bill wanted to wash his hands of the matter and get back to his own weekend. He went back to his room, back to the quiet.

Picking up the phone, he called down for room service. Yes, they could send up a large pot of black coffee, and a basket of hard rolls and butter. No, no eggs or meat, thanks anyway, he added. Okay, maybe a small glass of orange juice. It would keep him going until teatime when he'd take a break to indulge in some sandwiches, cakes and hot sweet tea. Dinner would then follow at seven-thirty again tonight. But tonight, he'd try to stay focused on why he was here this weekend and not on that redhead or the death of Mr. Smith.

He took off his sweater as the room was warming back up a bit now the electric was back on. He turned off the overhead chandelier, turned the desk lamp on, and set out his writing next to it, ready to get started as soon as the coffee arrived.

Bill sat in the desk chair and fingered the pages he had already written. He was too impatient to wait until after his late breakfast. The muse was already upon him, and he *had* to write. He picked up his pen and a fresh pad of paper and started in on what would be the best part of his weekend.

Epilogue

There would be nothing between them, there couldn't be. Ever. He was totally committed to his work, and she, well, she had other things on her mind. There would be the acquisition of worldly wealth and all those things her type of woman seemed to need: jewelry, clothes, diversions. He had no time for this.

He packed his leather suitcase with his only possessions. He would leave this place, this lady. Her red hair would call to him no longer. The scent of her expensive perfume would not beckon to him, twisting his heart around her will. He would go, and he would have to forget her.

A Very Sisterly Murder

Shelly Young Bell worked in industry as an Art Director and Director of Communications while also pursuing her writing. Most recently, she is the author of *The Phoenix Mysteries,* a series of novellas and short stories set near her home in Doylestown, PA. and *Stand Like the Brave*, a Historic Fiction book about a shell-shocked WW1 vet facing WW2.

Facebook: Shelly Young Bell, Mystery Writer
www.facebook.com/Shelly-Young-Bell-Mystery-Writer-100181952270650

Books by Shelly Young Bell

The Phoenix Detective Mysteries
A Very Sisterly Murder, Book 1
Murder at St. Katherine's, Book 2
The Diamond Dunes Murders, Book 3
The Cabot College Murders, Book 4
Population 10, The Dead End Murders, Book 5
R.S.V.P. to Murder, Book 6
Murder on the Promenade Deck, Book 7
Murder at 13 Curves, Book 8

Historic Novel
Stand Like the Brave

All available on Amazon under Shelly Young Bell

Shelly Young Bell

Made in the USA
Middletown, DE
06 November 2022

14301336R00052